# SARAH WEBB

## BEHIND CLOSED DOORS

Sarah Webb was born and lives in Dublin with her partner and young family. She was a children's bookseller for many years before becoming a full-time writer. She has written six best-selling novels, including *Always the Bridesmaid* and *It Had to Be You*. Her latest novel is *Take a Chance*.

Sarah also edited a collection of real-life travel adventures, *Travelling Light*, in aid of the Kisiizi Hospital in Uganda. She is very proud to be invlved in the Open Door series.

Find out more about Sarah on her website – www.sarahwebb.info

All royalties from the Irish sales of the Open Door series go to a charity of the author's choice. *Behind Closed Doors* royalties go to Kisiizi Hospital, Uganda.

NEW ISLAND *Open Door*

BEHIND CLOSED DOORS
First published 2006
by New Island
2 Brookside
Dundrum Road
Dublin 14

www.newisland.ie

A CIP catalogue record for this book is available from the British Library

ISBN 1 905494 03 3

New Island receives financial assistance from
The Arts Council (An Chomhairle Ealaíon), Dublin, Ireland.

Typeset by New Island
Printed in Ireland by ColourBooks
Cover design by Artmark

1 3 5 4 2

Dear Reader,

On behalf of myself and the other contributing authors, I would like to welcome you to the fifth Open Door series. We hope that you enjoy the books and that reading becomes a lasting pleasure in your life.

Warmest wishes,

*Patricia Scanlan.*

Patricia Scanlan
Series Editor

*To Ben, with all my love*

# One

Lunchtime and I was already stressed. I tapped my nails against the wheel of my car. Then I scowled at the learner driver in the old dark blue Ford Fiesta in front of me. He looked about fifteen. He was crawling along at just over twenty miles an hour. I muttered a swear word under my breath.

'You're not even supposed to be driving on your own,' I said, feeling silly as soon as the words had left my mouth. I was alone in the car. Talking to yourself was supposed to be the first sign of madness, after all.

The N11 was being dug up again for some hare-brained reason to do with drainage. This left only one lane of traffic on either side of the road. It was framed by hundreds of orange traffic cones and a host of bright-yellow-vested, bum-scratching workmen. There were also JCBs and steaming piles of hot, yet-to-be-laid tarmac.

My car stalled, stopping the traffic dead. The cars and lorries snaking behind me began to beep their horns – short parps at first, gradually getting longer and longer. Then the young man behind me decided to rest his hand on his loud air horn for several seconds, blasting me out of it. I jumped in my seat. I turned around and glared at him. He was wearing a dark suit and he looked like a sales rep. I bet he thought he was God's gift in his big saloon car and his greased-back hair.

'Men!' I muttered darkly and indicated left. I'd had enough. I was damned if I was going to sit in this terrible traffic for a moment longer. There was a garage just ahead of me. I'd turn the car around and use the back roads to Greystones. It was a longer drive, but at least I wouldn't have to sit in all this traffic.

I had to call in to a shop called Shoe Heaven in the village and grovel to the owner because someone in work had messed up. I worked as a freelance journalist for an Irish fashion magazine called *Ruby*. But more about that in a minute.

It also meant I could call into my best friend Cathy's baby shower. Cathy was five months pregnant. She was having a lunch party to celebrate. She'd insisted on having it in her own house. Cathy loved entertaining. If I had her house, I would too.

Cathy lived in Kilcoole, just outside Greystones, with her husband and two children. I wasn't exactly looking forward to the lunch party. Some of Cathy's friends were … there's no nice way to put this … wagons with a capital W. Horribly smug women who looked down their perfectly formed noses at women like me. Women who work.

They were professional 'mommies' who thought the world revolved around them and the other 'mommies' in their group. They really were awful.

As I drove along the leafy back roads, my mobile rang. I grabbed it from the passenger seat, clicked it on and held it to my ear.

'Hello? Yes?' I said.

'Are you all right?' the voice on the other end asked. It was Anita, one of my oldest friends. Anita used to be a journalist like me but now she works in a bookshop. Sounds sweet and stress free, doesn't it, working in a bookshop? Well, according to Anita, it really isn't. It's all about maths apparently. How many of this or that title you can sell and at what price. And she never gets to read at work, much to her disgust. But she did get to meet Maeve Binchy at a book launch in her shop. She said Maeve was even nicer in real life.

'You sound a little stressed,' said Anita.

'Oh, sorry,' I said with a sigh. 'I've just had one of those mornings. I have to be in Shoe Heaven before twelve. Nora at the magazine borrowed some pink Gucci suede boots from the shop for a fashion shoot. And then she wore them to a party at the weekend, the big idiot. She ruined them. The heels are all scuffed and the soles are dirty.

They're going to go mad. So I have to apologise in person and offer them a free ad.'

'How much are they worth?'

'Too much. Don't ask! I could kill Nora. And then I have to go to Cathy's house for that baby-shower lunch thing.'

'Amy, it's ten past one.'

'Tell me about it. Listen, I need your help. Do you have a second?'

'Sure, fire ahead. But should you be talking and driving at the same time?' Anita asked with concern.

'Of course not.' I tried not to snap. I didn't have time for this. 'But the road's pretty quiet and I'm not changing gears or anything. And I'm running so late …' I sighed deeply. I hoped Anita would take pity on me and drop the subject. Anita was a stickler for the rules. Talking on your mobile while driving was a no-no in her book.

'What happened to that hands-free kit I bought you?' she asked.

I ignored her. It was still sitting in its box on my desk, buried somewhere under the magazines, newspaper clippings and general work mess.

'Anita, I promised Kitty a three-thousand-word article by the day after tomorrow for the July edition.' Kitty was the editor of *Ruby*. She was a strong, ambitious woman who was only twenty-six, a year younger than me. She had clawed her way to the top of her profession and intended to stay there. She wasn't an easy woman to work for. She scared me sometimes. She had a habit of creeping up behind me when I was typing. Or checking out websites. Or e-mailing Anita. Especially when I was e-mailing Anita.

'An article on what?' asked Anita.

'That's the problem. I haven't a clue.

She wants something glitzy and "now". Maybe an interview with a designer, something about shoes, sex … Oh, I don't know. I'm all out of ideas. That's why I need your help. Have you any ideas for me? Anything at all – I'm desperate!'

# Two

Anita thought for a moment. As an ex-journalist, she was good at ideas. She read the newspapers and the gossip magazines religiously. 'How about an interview with Steve Kenny? I read in this morning's paper that he's over from London at the moment. His new collection is creating quite a stir. All those naked breasts, see-through tops and everything.' Steve Kenny was a young Irish designer who was talented, good looking, single and straight.

'Did him in January.'

'A feature on Beth Goggin's new

crime novel? She's only nineteen and her father is a friend of Bono's. Might be interesting.'

'Kitty interviewed her in March. And I did her for *U* magazine when her last book came out.'

'Oh, yes, I'd forgotten about that. Um, the Pink Fashion Ball?'

'Did it in May.'

'What about that glam celebrity chef – Harry Winton? He's in Dublin this week promoting his new book.' Anita was refusing to admit defeat. Harry was the new Jamie Oliver, but even better looking. He was all floppy black hair and whiter-than-white teeth. Anita was a genius.

'Brilliant! Any ideas on how I'd contact him?'

'Lou Lou Brady represents Harry's publishers. I can give you her number. She might be able to set something up.

She owes me one – I gave her spot prizes for the Red Letter Ball in aid of The Children's Hospital last autumn.'

'Anita, you're a genius! Harry would be perfect. And I met Lou Lou at one of the book launches in your shop recently. Nice woman. I'll ring her right now. Hang on, I need to pull in and grab a pen to take down her number.'

'You could key it straight into your mobile,' Anita pointed out.

'I could, if I was mobile literate, but I'm not,' I reminded her. 'I haven't worked out how to do that yet without cutting you off. And anyway, I'm driving, remember?'

'I'll explain anyway,' Anita said. 'It's a useful skill to have. It's easy, you just …'

'Another time. Thanks for your help. I'm going to ring Lou Lou as soon as you give me the number.'

# Three

'Lou Lou, it's Amy O'Brien, Anita's friend,' I said.

'Hi, Amy, how can I help you?' Lou Lou came straight to the point. Like me, she was a busy woman.

'I'd like to interview Harry Winton for the July issue of *Ruby*. Any slots free?'

'Plenty. But I should tell you, *Joy* are doing a feature on him for their July issue. Is that a problem?'

Damn, I thought. I should have got in earlier. *Joy* was another Irish

women's magazine, *Ruby*'s main rival.
'Has Harry already done the interview?' I asked Lou Lou.

'Yes, on Monday. With Valerie
Powell. They're doing a three-page
spread. They're using a photograph of
him on the cover.'

I was about to swear but I bit my
tongue. 'That's a pity. But I'm afraid I
can't do Harry then. Anyone else
around?'

Lou Lou thought for a second. 'I
probably shouldn't tell you this, but
Rex O'Hara's new film is opening
tomorrow tonight in the Savoy.'

'Is he in Dublin?' I asked. Now this
was interesting. Rex was one of
Ireland's biggest rising stars. He was a
local boy made good in Hollywood and
the darling of the media. They were
calling him the next Colin Farrell.
Unusually for a movie star, Rex was
polite and well mannered. He was also

a classically trained actor and devastatingly handsome – a killer combination.

'Yes. I can't promise anything. His diary is packed, but leave it with me. I'll get back to you within the hour, OK?'

'I really appreciate this, Lou Lou,' I said. 'Thanks.'

'No problem. Talk to you later.'

I clicked off my phone and breathed a sigh of relief. Rex O'Hara. If only I could pull this one off, then the staff job at *Ruby* would be in the bag. You see, I wanted to buy a house with my long-suffering boyfriend, Joe. But banks didn't look too kindly on freelancers like me. Joe was an electrician and he'd just gone out on his own. So his bank statements didn't look all that healthy either, unfortunately.

We'd been together for nearly five years. And we both wanted somewhere we could call our own. My mum wasn't too thrilled at the idea. She kept saying, 'Why don't you get married first, Amy? Before buying a house.' But I wasn't ready to get married. I was only twenty-seven, after all.

Joe had dropped the odd hint all right. He was mad about his nieces and nephews. I knew he'd like a family of his own. But whatever about getting married, I really wasn't ready to be a mum yet!

Joe and I lived in a rented apartment in Donnybrook. A nice enough apartment, but it wasn't ours. What we really wanted was a little house near the sea – in Shankill or Bray, maybe. We'd both had enough of town living. It was time to move out to the suburbs.

Joe wanted to buy an old place and do it up. He was a dab hand with a power drill and was itching to get stuck into a project. I had no interest in DIY. But I was looking forward to putting my own stamp on the interior.

And I couldn't wait to hit my favourite auction house, Buckley's in Sandycove. I'd covered it for the magazine recently. The article was called 'How to Find Cheap Chic Furniture in Dublin'. It was a fascinating day. Some of the old furniture was dirt cheap – especially the larger pieces. They just wouldn't fit in apartments and new houses, the auctioneer had explained.

I'd even bought a battered old oil painting with an ornate gold frame. It was a bit worse for wear. I'd managed to transform it into a stunning mirror with gold spray paint and a piece of glass from Woodie's. All I needed now was the fireplace to put it over.

I knew I was more than ready to buy my own place. I didn't want to leave it too late. I needed to get my foot on the property ladder. The staff job at *Ruby* was just what the doctor, or should I say the bank manager, ordered.

I checked in my rear-view mirror and moved away from the side of the road. I was *so* late for Cathy's lunch thing. But I'd promised to make an appearance so I thought I'd better get moving. Luckily I was only ten minutes away from Kilcoole Woods, the housing estate where Cathy lived. I'd drop the shoes into Shoe Heaven, make my apologies and be at Cathy's a few minutes later. Perfect.

It was always a struggle keeping in contact with Cathy. We lived such different lives. Cathy married Arthur Ryan when she was only twenty-three. Cathy was the first of my close friends to get married. In fact, most of my other friends were still single.

Cathy met Arthur at work. She had completed a year at beauty college before taking a secretarial course. She'd landed a good, steady job as a receptionist at an auctioneer's, O'Kelly and Sons. She met Arthur there. Arthur was an ambitious man almost ten years older than Cathy. Apparently he was 'on the fast track for success' according to Cathy, whatever that meant.

Cathy left her job as soon as she got pregnant. She dutifully produced two children in quick succession. They were blond-haired dotes called Arthur and Anna. Arthur was named after his father and his grandfather before him. But I always found it a bit confusing.

Anita and Cathy had never got on. Anita found Cathy very smug. Cathy couldn't understand Anita's reluctance to find a husband and settle down. The three of us did meet for lunch occasionally, but Cathy and Anita always ended up arguing. And keeping the peace was exhausting.

I pulled up outside Shoe Heaven on double yellow lines and put on my hazard lights. I didn't want any passing guard to think I intended to park there for long. I stepped out of the car and walked around to the passenger side. I took the pink-and-white-striped shoe-box off the seat.

I took a deep breath and walked into the shop.

'Yes?' A tall woman with a long, pointy nose stared at me. Her grey hair was scraped back off her face. Her red lipstick looked like a slash of blood on her pale, moon-like face.

'Are you Ellen, the owner?' I asked nervously.

She nodded. 'Yes, why?'

'I'm Amy,' I said. 'From *Ruby* magazine. I'm just returning the boots you kindly loaned us for the "Pretty in Pink" fashion shoot.' I handed her the box. 'The boots got a little damaged during the shoot. I'm terribly sorry.'

Ellen opened the box, took a boot out and studied it. She sucked in her breath dramatically when she saw the black scuff-marks on the heels. 'So I see,' she said. 'Have you any idea how much these boots cost?'

'Yes,' I said quickly. 'And to make up for it we want to offer you a free ad in the next edition of the magazine.'

Ellen looked at me and cocked her head to one side. 'A full page ad?' she asked.

I wasn't in the mood to argue with her. I was very late for Cathy's lunch. 'Yes, yes,' I said.

'Fine,' she said, putting the boot

back in the box. 'And you may as well keep them now. They're no good to me like that. I can't sell them.'

I was shocked. They were amazing boots. That's why Nora had borrowed them in the first place. 'Really? I can have them?'

Ellen smiled at me. A smile that lit up her face. I realised that she was a lot younger than I'd originally thought. 'I have far too many pairs of boots already,' she said. 'I'd have nowhere to put them.' She handed me the box. 'Go on. They're yours.'

I grinned at her. 'You've just made my day.' I skipped out of the shop, happy to be alive. That would teach Nora for making me do her dirty work.

But my mood changed as soon as I approached Cathy's house.

# Four

I pulled up outside Cathy's house at exactly twenty past one. The road outside the house was littered with an assortment of large family cars and jeeps. Each had car seats and bright pink or light blue 'baby on board' stickers.

I always wondered what exactly those stickers meant. Beware, driver likely to swerve at any moment. Or maybe, beware, driver likely to ask you extremely personal questions. Like:

When are you getting married?

When are you thinking of starting a family?

Isn't it a shame you're still single? Would you like to meet my cousin Fred? He has a bit of a BO problem, but he's available and beggars can't be choosers.

I parked behind an old Range Rover and took a deep breath. I looked at the pink-and-white box on my passenger seat and then down at my grubby old white runners. The boots were my size, 5. And they'd make me a lot more confident. And let's face it: I was dying for an excuse to wear them. So I pulled off my runners and pulled on the boots. The suede was as soft as butter against the skin of my calves. The boots stopped just under my knee and looked amazing. God bless Nora! Not that I was going to tell her what had happened, or she might claim them as her own. Nora was like that. They were far too nice for nosey Nora, as we called her in the office. I'd keep them for myself. For special occasions. Like facing Cathy's awful friends, for example.

I grabbed the bottle of wine and my bag from the floor on the passenger side. The bottle had been rolling around while I drove, but luckily it hadn't broken. Then I locked the car. Not that I needed to. No one was likely to steal my heap of junk.

As I walked towards Cathy's house, I heard yells from the front garden. I looked over. Arthur Junior was wetting two larger boys with the garden hose. I smiled. Nothing had changed. Good old Arthur, always in trouble. The boys were dressed in white linen shorts and carefully pressed light-blue shirts. I just knew that their mother wouldn't be too amused at her little darlings' wet clothes.

Arthur, as usual, was completely naked. At four, he was a little old to be constantly naked, and Cathy hated it. She spent her days running after him, begging him to at least put some shorts on. But Arthur was a stubborn little fellow and always ripped his clothes off at every opportunity. He was only ever fully dressed in his father's presence. The four-year-old loved his food and was a bit on the chubby side. His little tummy wobbled as he ran around. But this just made me love him even more.

'Hi, Arthur,' I grinned. 'How are things?'

Arthur looked at me, at the hose and then back at me.

'Don't even think about it,' I said. 'I have something for you in my bag. Don't tell your mum, OK?'

Arthur nodded eagerly, dropped the hose at his feet and ran towards me.

His wet blond hair splattered water all over the path.

'Hi, Amy,' he said, giving me a wide, toothy smile. He stared at my bag and licked his lips.

I laughed. 'Expecting something to eat?' I asked.

He nodded eagerly. I was his godmother, and I always brought him a treat when I visited. Cathy always gave out to me for it. Arthur was only allowed sweets on Saturdays. Even then he had to wash his teeth carefully afterwards. This took most of the fun out of eating them, if you ask me. She was even talking about putting him on a diet, poor child. He was only four, for heaven's sake. And he was very active. He'd run off the baby fat in no time, I kept telling her. It was one of the few things myself and Arthur Senior agreed on.

I dug my hand into my red leather bag and pulled out a packet of Starburst, Arthur's favourites.

'Here you go.' I handed them over and smiled at his obvious delight.

'Thanks, Amy.' He threw his arms around my legs and gave me an almighty hug.

'You're welcome, pet.' I removed his arms and looked towards the front door.

Cathy was standing on the doorstep, her arms folded in front of her chest, with a serious expression on her face.

'Into the back garden, Arthur. Now!' she said firmly. 'And you can hand over those sweets on your way.'

'Aw, Mum!'

'Don't argue with me, young man. You're in enough trouble as it is for wetting the Murphy brothers. Their mum is not impressed.'

'Can I just have one sweet, please? Amy gave them to me. Please?'

'Just one,' Cathy said sternly.

He opened the packet quickly in case she changed her mind. He took out a sweet, unwrapped it and jammed it into his mouth. Then he reluctantly handed Cathy the rest of the packet.

'Oh dear,' I murmured. 'Sorry, Arthur. Caught in the act. Didn't mean to get you in trouble.' I ruffled his damp hair and patted him gently on the back as he walked past me. 'Off you go.'

He toddled off happily down the side of the house towards the back garden, with his mouth jammed full of fruity flavour. I knew I was in for a grilling.

# Five

'Hi, Cathy,' I said a little too brightly. I leant over, kissed my friend on the cheek and thrust the bottle of wine into her hands. She looked tired. There were faint purple shadows under her eyes and her skin was pale. I thought it better not to mention it. It might make her feel even worse.

'Thanks,' Cathy said. 'But I've asked you before not to give Arthur sweets. It ruins his routine, not to mention his teeth.'

'Sorry,' I said, but I wasn't sorry at all. The odd treat now and then wasn't going to kill him. 'I'll try to remember next time. Now where's the food? I'm starving.'

Cathy stood back and allowed me to walk inside. As soon as I entered, loud screams came from the living-room.

'Who's strangling the cat?' I asked.

Cathy glared at me. 'Simon Kelly's teething. It's hardly his fault, poor lamb.'

'I suppose not,' I said. Cathy seemed to be in a right old mood. It was safer to humour her. 'The hall looks lovely. I like the cream. Very classy.'

'The painter only left yesterday,' said Cathy. 'Do you really like it? I'm not sure. It's very plain, isn't it?'

'I really like it,' I reassured her. 'It just needs a couple of pictures to brighten it up. It'll be perfect then.'

Cathy smiled at me gratefully. 'You're right. That's just what it needs. A few pictures.'

Just then two toddlers dashed past us, limbs flailing. I curved my body backwards to avoid their little waving arms.

'More kids,' I said, then laughed. 'Oops, forgot to bring mine.'

Cathy went quiet for a moment. She had a strange expression on her face. I couldn't quite read it.

'Cathy?' I asked. 'Are you OK? What's wrong?'

'Did I forget to tell you?'

'Tell me what?'

'Most of the women here are my Tiny Tots friends.'

'What's Tiny Tots?' I asked in confusion.

'You know – the mother and baby club I'm in. We meet in the local

community centre once a week and ...'
She stopped when she saw my face. 'I
didn't warn you, did I?'

'No, you didn't. You said it was a
baby shower, Cathy. I was expecting
grown-up food, not mashed-up carrots
and puréed apple.'

'There's normal food as well,' she
said quietly.

I stared at her. 'Does everyone here
have a baby with them?'

Cathy nodded. 'Or a toddler.'

'What were you thinking?' I said.
'You practically begged me to come
along.'

'I know, but I really want to talk to
you about something. You're always so
busy at the weekends.' Cathy began to
play with the ends of her hair nervously.
'We have such different lives these days.
It's so hard with two kids and everything
and the new one on the way ...'

I put my arm around Cathy's shoulders. She was obviously upset about something and I wasn't helping. What kind of friend was I?

'Not to worry, Cathy,' I said kindly. 'I'll stay for a little bit and we can talk.'

Cathy smiled at me gratefully. 'Thanks. I really appreciate it. Maybe you'll even enjoy it.'

'Maybe.' I attempted a smile. I'd met some of Cathy's Tiny Tots friends before. They weren't exactly impressed by my childless state. In fact, one of them, a woman called Lisa, who had been a year behind us in school, had been positively hostile towards me. Last time I'd met her, she had asked did I want children. Quite a personal question, I'm sure you will agree. I told her that my career came first for the moment. And I said that I had no intention of breeding quite yet, thanks very much. I was only just twenty-seven. What was the rush?

But Lisa, as you can imagine, wasn't amused.

'Having children makes you a better person,' she'd said. 'Far less selfish. It's been the making of me,' she continued. 'Felix and Lizzie are the best things that have ever happened to me.' She smiled smugly. 'Being a mother has made me whole as a person.'

If Cathy hadn't been there, I would have argued with her. But sometimes it's not worth the trouble.

So, as long as Lisa wasn't at Cathy's lunch, I could just about cope.

# Six

'Come into the kitchen and get yourself something to eat,' said Cathy.

I was starving. I didn't have to be asked twice.

Once in the kitchen, Cathy handed me a large dark-blue pottery plate.

'These are nice,' I said, tapping the plate with my finger. It gave a hollow ping. 'New?'

Cathy nodded. 'Yes, they're from the Avoca shop. Do you really like them?'

'Sure. They're a great colour.'

'Do you honestly like them or are you just being kind?'

I looked at Cathy. She was being very odd. 'They're just plates.'

She blushed. 'Sorry, yes, I know. Help yourself to salads and bread.' She pointed at the table, which was full of plates and bowls of delicious-looking food. 'And there's homemade pizza slices and chicken pie on the sideboard. And there's chocolate cake for dessert. The carrot sticks and sandwiches in the shape of animals are for the children. But you can have some if you like.'

I smiled. 'You've gone to a lot of trouble.' I began to heap some potato salad onto my plate. Maybe this lunch wasn't going to be so bad after all. At least I'd get well fed.

'Hello, Amy.' A tall woman dressed in a white linen top and perfectly pressed matching trousers glided towards me. Her long black hair was tied back in a neat ponytail, a few wispy bits framing her pale oval face. My heart sank.

'Hi, Lisa,' I said evenly. 'How nice to see you again.' I plastered a fake smile on my face.

'How's work?' Lisa wrinkled her nose as she said 'work', as if the word alone was distasteful.

'Fine, thanks,' I replied. 'And how are the twins?'

'Very well, thank you. Felix has just started French lessons and little Lizzie is taking ballet, Irish and Greek dancing. Good to expand their cultural sides, don't you think?'

'Quite.' As the twins were only just four, Lisa was clearly throwing her money away. But who was I to judge? After all, Lisa had married money. Her husband was Jim O'Hare, a property developer twenty years her senior.

I wasn't sure what to say next, so I said nothing. Lisa immediately filled the silence.

'And what are you working on at the moment? Still freelancing in the fashion world? Or have you managed to move on yet?' Lisa gave me a sickly smile. 'Must be annoying. Stuck in a rut like that.'

'Still in fashion,' I said. I refused to let her get to me. 'I spent all morning arranging shoes for photographs. Nothing terribly glamorous. Of course, I did get to try them all on. And they were stunning. All the latest ranges for autumn from Italy, France, Spain … boring really.'

Lisa raised her eyebrows. I knew she shared my love of shoes. We'd talked about it the last time we'd met. It was pretty much the only thing we both had in common. 'Really?' she asked.

'But you wouldn't be interested in something as boring as shoes, now would you, Lisa? The Jimmy Choos and Manolo Blahniks of this world are so frightfully boring, darling.'

With that, I turned towards Cathy, who was listening to our conversation open-mouthed. 'Now, Cathy, you had something to ask me?' I asked pointedly.

Cathy thought for a moment. 'Yes, it was about a dinner I have to attend. I wanted some advice on what to wear.'

'I'll see you later, Cathy.' Lisa was well aware that she'd been snubbed. She swept out of the patio doors into the garden.

'Did you have to be so rude to Lisa?' Cathy asked me. She was biting her lip nervously. She hated upsetting anyone.

'Yes!' I said. 'Did you hear what she said about my career? Silly cow.'

Cathy sighed. 'Don't let it get to you. She's just jealous. She'd love your job, you know. I think she's a little bored, to tell the truth.'

'It can't be easy looking after two children with only one nanny and a housekeeper,' I said.

'Don't be so sarcastic. It doesn't suit you,' Cathy said.

'Sorry, I'm just tired. It's been one hell of a week.'

'Tell me all about it. I want to hear everything. I've had such a boring week.'

I opened my mouth to say something. But before I got a word out I was interrupted.

'Cathy, have you got a cloth?' A red-faced woman came running towards us. 'Little Harry has had a little accident, I'm afraid.'

'That's OK, Jen,' Cathy assured her. 'It's nothing to worry about. Boys are like that.'

'Potty training,' the woman mouthed to me. I really didn't want to know.

While Cathy was helping her, my mobile rang. I excused myself and moved into the hall to answer it.

# Seven

'Amy. Bad news, I'm afraid,' Lou Lou said on the other end of the phone.

'Oh?' I said.

'Rex is completely booked up for the whole day and night. And he's not doing any interviews tomorrow as he's spending the day with his family. Sorry. I gave it my best shot.'

'Not to worry. Thanks for trying.'

'Not at all. Talk to you soon. Must dash. Bye.'

I clicked off my mobile. What the hell am I going to do now? I thought.

I went back into the kitchen, but Cathy had disappeared. I decided to eat. After a full plate of salad, I tucked into the desserts. I sat and ate on my own, surrounded by children's screams and cries. Then I decided to be brave. I walked into the living-room.

'Hi, I'm Polly,' the dark-haired woman on the sofa said, moving over to let me sit down. Even sitting down she looked tall. She had a cluster of freckles around her button nose. She spoke with a strong accent, but I couldn't quite place it. Dutch, maybe, or German. 'And that's Molly.' She pointed to the blonde-haired girl who was dressing a Barbie doll on the floor in front of them. The child was wearing denim dungarees and a red jumper, just like her mother. 'She's nearly four.'

Polly and Molly? I looked at the woman's face for any trace of irony, but found none.

'Hi, I'm Amy. I'm a friend of Cathy's.'

'And which is yours?' Polly asked.

'Excuse me?'

'Child. Which one is yours?'

'I don't actually have any children,' I said.

'Really?' Polly said, raising her eyebrows. So what are you doing here, her expression said. I felt very out of place.

'I'll just go and help Cathy with the food.' I jumped up and made my way back into the kitchen.

'Are you all right?' Cathy asked me. 'You look a little flustered.'

'I shouldn't have stayed,' I said. 'I'm sick of being asked where my children are. I haven't had a normal conversation yet.'

'What's normal?' Cathy asked with a smile. 'It's just different, that's all. Not what you're used to.'

'Maybe.'

'Anyway, you can't go yet. I haven't had a chance to talk to you properly. Please stay.'

I glanced at my watch. Cathy was right. I hadn't been there very long. It would be rude to leave so quickly – even if I wasn't exactly enjoying myself. 'OK. I'll stay for half an hour. But that's it.'

'Great. I'll introduce you to Pam. You'll like her. She's very normal. She's keeping an eye on Anna for me.'

Pam was sitting outside with some of the other mothers, including the dreaded Lisa. Lisa looked up, caught my eye and looked away again. How rude!

'Pam,' Cathy said. 'This is Amy. We're old friends. Amy writes for *Ruby* magazine.'

'Hey, less of the old,' I laughed.

'Nice to meet you, Amy.' Pam

smiled up at me, shielding her eyes from the sun. She had shoulder-length dark brown hair and a friendly looking face. Little Anna was sitting on her knee. 'And you know Anna.'

'Of course. And which are your children?'

Pam waved her hand at the back of the garden, where several youngsters were playing on the wooden climbing frame and slide. 'Dan and Sally are over there somewhere, but let's not talk about them. Cathy's told me all about your job, of course. She's very proud of you. It sounds fascinating. Sit down and tell me all about it. I'm so deprived of adult conversation these days. I used to be a journalist for one of the daily newspapers and I really miss it.'

I was only too delighted. I began to tell Pam about some of the recent fashion pieces I'd written or styled. She seemed genuinely interested and was a great listener.

'I'll be back in a moment,' Cathy said, delighted that the two of us seemed to be hitting it off.

'Two journalists in one garden,' Lisa called over from the chair where she was sitting. 'That must be a first for Tiny Tots.'

'What would you call a group of journalists?' the small fine-boned woman beside her asked. It was Lisa's 'best friend', Millie. She'd also been at our school, in the same class as Lisa. I couldn't get away from them. They'd been horrible in school. Bullies. They'd made some of the quieter girls' lives a misery. And from what I could make out, they were still horrible now.

'A gaggle?' Lisa suggested.

'I'll think you'll find that's geese,' Pam said mildly.

'How about a gossip of journalists?' I suggested.

'Oh, very clever, Amy,' Lisa smiled. But the smile stopped at her lips and never reached her eyes. 'How about a scum of journalists?'

Pam looked at me and back at Lisa. 'And what about us mums? A comfort of mums?'

'Oh, but we're not all mothers here, are we?' Lisa pointed out.

'Do you have a problem with that?' I asked sharply.

Pam put her hand on mine. 'I think you're very lucky, personally. I'd love to have some of my own time back – and a job. I never thought I'd say it, but I miss working.'

'I certainly don't,' Millie sniffed. 'Highly overrated, work.'

'Surely not,' Pam said. 'Not if you find a job you really like. And besides, looking after children *is* work. It's much harder than my job ever was. Isn't it?'

Lisa and Millie nodded but said nothing. They both had full-time nannies. I decided not to point this out. I was bigger than that.

'How's Daisy's lovely boyfriend, Millie?' Pam asked, anxious to change the subject. 'He's doing really well for himself these days. I loved *Bright Water*. He was brilliant in that.'

'Rex is fine,' Millie said. 'Very busy, of course, with the new film. The première is tomorrow night and he's up to ninety with interviews and photo calls. We haven't seen much of him or Daisy this trip.'

'You know Rex O'Hara?' I asked in amazement.

'Yes.' Millie smiled at me. She had a smug look on her face. 'Didn't you know? He's engaged to my sister, Daisy.'

'No. I had no idea.'

'They've been together for three years now. But they keep their personal lives to themselves. The whole Hollywood thing can get very intrusive otherwise – everyone knowing your business.'

'I suppose so,' I said. 'Where did she meet him? Have they been together long?'

Millie sighed. 'Let's not talk about all that. Other people's love lives are very boring, don't you think?'

'Not at all,' I insisted. 'In fact, I was hoping to interview him for *Ruby*. Maybe you could ask him for me. It wouldn't take long – just some questions and a quick photo. I'd be really grateful. I asked his publicist but I left it too late.'

Millie stared at me. 'Let's just forget you said that, will we?'

'So rude,' Lisa added. 'Really, Amy, have you no manners?'

'I don't see what the problem is,' I said. 'I just asked if Millie wouldn't mind ...'

'Let's just drop it,' Lisa said, cutting me off. 'Better that way. So Pam, how's the pregnancy coming along? Any morning sickness?'

I was mortified. Maybe I shouldn't have asked for Millie's help. But this was Dublin, for goodness sake, not Hollywood. In Dublin people helped each other out. And it was the media that had made Rex O'Hara the superstar that he was today. In fact, one of his very first media interviews was published in *Ruby*.

I tried not to think about Lisa's putdown as I studied Pam's stomach. It was certainly gently rounded. But I honestly hadn't noticed she was pregnant.

'No, thank goodness,' Pam replied. 'I'm feeling great.'

'How pregnant are you?' I asked. I thought I should try to show some interest.

'Nearly six months.'

'Wow, you look great, so slim.'

'That's not always a good thing, Amy,' Lisa said. 'It can mean that the baby isn't developing properly. It can mean there's something wrong.'

I stared at Lisa. What a horrible thing to say.

'But in this case it's fine, Lisa,' Pam said firmly. 'The baby is very healthy, thank you very much.'

'I didn't mean to suggest …'

'I'm sure you didn't,' Pam interrupted. 'You'd never do anything like that, would you, Lisa?'

'Um, what's Rex's new film about, Millie?' I gabbled, clutching at straws. Cathy would be upset if she found us all fighting. 'Have you seen it yet? Is it good?'

'Is this on the record?' Millie's eyes narrowed.

'Of course not, I was just wondering.'

'I don't think I can divulge anything about *Land's End*,' Millie said with a sniff. 'Just in case. You'll have to see it at the cinema like everyone else.'

'Right,' I said, tight-lipped. I'd had enough of trying to keep the peace and be 'nice'. Lisa and Millie deserved to be horse-whipped. 'So Pam, do you like my new boots?' I held out my foot and Pam gasped in admiration.

'They are beautiful,' she said. 'Are they Gucci?'

'Yes, well spotted. I got them free,' I said. 'Isn't that great? There are some perks to working for a fashion magazine.'

Lisa and Millie looked at my boots enviously. Ha! I knew it was petty, but I didn't care.

'So how are you all getting on?' Cathy asked as she walked back into the garden.

'Oh, just great,' I lied. 'Aren't we, girls? Just like one big happy family.'

# Eight

Twenty minutes later, I was sitting on the bed in Cathy's room. She'd finally got away from the mad mothers who kept asking her for things for their children. Honestly, it would put you off having children for good.

'So, what's up?' I asked. 'What's this dinner you're going to?'

Cathy sighed deeply. 'That was just to shut Lisa up. There's no dinner. I wish there was. I could do with a bit of excitement.' She looked down at her hands, which were clasped on her lap.

'Amy, I'm bored out of my tree,' she admitted. 'I love Arthur and Anna to bits, but I'm going nuts. I spend my time looking for things to do to fill my days. I'm sick to the teeth of shopping and bloody Tiny Tots. I feel like I'm losing my personality. I need your help.'

'Right.' I was taken aback. I hadn't expected this.

'After I have this baby, I want to retrain as a baby masseuse. Do you think I'm crazy?'

'Baby masseuse,' I said. 'Is there such a thing?'

Cathy nodded eagerly. 'I loved massage in beauty college. I was pretty good at it too. I used to practise on you, remember? It was part of my course.'

I had a vague recollection of having my back rolled and pummelled by an over-eager Cathy many years ago. 'Yes, I think so.'

'There's a course in Rathmines for people with some former qualifications. It's three evenings a week for six weeks. After that, you can set up your own classes. There's a huge demand for baby massage, apparently. I've talked to two different health nurses and my GP. They are all really positive about the effects on a crying baby and ...' Cathy bubbled on about the benefits of baby massage while I tried to look interested. I hadn't seen Cathy this animated about anything for a long time. Not since the big charity ball she'd organised in the RDS.

'Sounds fascinating,' I said. 'But what does Arthur think?'

'He loves being messaged and he thinks Mummy should ...'

'Arthur Senior. You know, your husband.'

Cathy blushed. 'I haven't actually told him yet. But he might not be too keen on the whole idea. He wants to have another baby after this one. He says four children is the perfect family. But I don't think I can go through all this again, Amy. I'm exhausted. I want my body back. I feel like I've been invaded by aliens.'

I laughed out loud. I couldn't help it. 'Sorry,' I said, 'I didn't mean to laugh.'

'That's OK. But what am I going to do? Arthur is serious about having another baby after bump is born.' Cathy rubbed her large belly and sighed.

'Is he now?' I raised my eyebrows. 'That would certainly be a miracle of modern science.'

'You know what I mean.' Cathy sighed again. 'I just want to do something for myself, Amy. Earn my own money. Spend some time on my own again. I'd like to get this baby out of the way, then go back to work when it's a little bigger. Arthur's mum has already said she'd help out a few mornings a week. I suppose I might think about having another baby some time in the future, but not right now. At the moment, I feel like I'm just Arthur's wife and the kids' mother. I want to be me.'

'Reminds me of Toyah Wilcox,' I smiled. 'Remember her?'

'With the orange hair?'

'Correct.' I sang a few bars of the song 'I Want to Be Free'.

Cathy made a face. 'Never could sing, could you?'

I elbowed her in the side. 'Thanks. So what are you going to do about the baby massage? Are you going to take the course?'

Cathy shrugged. 'I'm not sure. What do you think?'

'Talk to Arthur. Explain how you feel. You might be surprised. He's a reasonable man and he adores you. He might surprise you.'

'When exactly?' Cathy asked. 'He's always working. I'm in bed before he comes in most evenings. The weekends are spent doing boring house things like shopping and gardening. But I'd like to do the course before the baby is born. Even if I don't set up classes straight away, it will come in useful with the new baby. And I could just about fit the six-week course in before I pop.'

'Why don't you go away for a weekend together without the kids?' I said. 'Before the baby is born. Talk about it.'

'I wish,' Cathy sighed. 'Who'd mind them? Mum can't cope with them for more than a few hours. Arthur's parents are always busy playing golf at the weekends.'

I thought for a moment. 'I'll do it,' I said. 'I'll move into the house for the weekend and look after them. How about next weekend? No time like the present and all that.'

'I can't ask you to do that,' Cathy protested. 'You're always so busy. And what about Joe?'

'If it's OK by you, he could stay here too. He's brilliant with kids. And we'd both enjoy a weekend in the country.'

'Hardly the country,' Cathy snorted.

'It is to us.' I smiled. 'Compared to Donnybrook, it's the sticks.'

'Are you serious about next week-end?' Cathy asked, her eyes lighting up. 'Because I could book somewhere and surprise Arthur. He's not as busy as usual at the moment. If I found some-where with a swimming pool and a good restaurant, I know he'd be delighted. He's not usually a man for surprises. But a weekend in a hotel without the kids ...' Cathy grinned. 'Now that would be the best surprise he's had in a long time.'

'Go ahead and book,' I said. 'I'll check with Joe. But I'm sure he won't mind one little bit.'

Cathy threw her arms around me and gave me a big hug. Her bump got in the way. We both laughed.

'I can't thank you enough,' she said.

'It's only one weekend,' I smiled. I was delighted to be able to help. And in a funny way I was quite looking forward to it. I could spoil Arthur and Anna to my heart's content.

'Now we'd better go downstairs,' Cathy said. 'My guests will wonder where I am. And I think some of them have presents for me.'

My heart sank. A present for the mum to be. Of course! Why hadn't I thought of that?

As we walked down the stairs, Cathy patted my arm. 'You brought me wine, remember?' she said, reading my mind. 'And a weekend without Arthur and Anna. No one can beat that.'

'Oh, but I'm sure Lisa will try,' I said.

Cathy laughed. 'Shush!'

# Nine

When Cathy walked into the living-room, all the mothers started clapping and cheering. It was quite sweet really and Cathy was delighted.

Lisa stood up and hushed the crowd. 'We're here today to wish you all the best with the rest of your pregnancy, Cathy, and the new baby. And as a token of our good wishes, we have some presents for you.'

Cathy smiled and waved her hands in the air. 'You shouldn't have.'

'We wanted to,' Pam said, smiling back. 'Really. Cathy, sit down before you fall down.'

'Where are all the kids?' Cathy asked, looking around. Apart from the odd baby and younger toddler, most of the children had disappeared.

'My nanny, Barbara, is here to help out,' Lisa said. 'She brought Millie's nanny with her. We thought it would give us a few blissful child-free minutes.'

'Thanks, girls.' Cathy blew kisses at Lisa and Millie.

I sat down on the arm of the sofa, next to Pam.

'I'll go first,' Lisa said.

'Surprise, surprise,' Pam whispered to me.

Lisa handed Cathy a square present. It was beautifully wrapped in dark pink tissue paper with a thick white ribbon tied around it.

'Go on,' Lisa said. 'Open it.'

Cathy untied the ribbon and tore open the tissue. Inside was a tiny pair of baby boots. They were sky blue with a little white cloud pattern on the soft leather.

'Oh, Lisa,' Cathy said. 'They're lovely. Thanks.' She gave Lisa a kiss on the cheek.

'You're welcome. I got them in Spain. We were in Madrid the weekend before last.'

'Me next, me next,' Millie said. She handed over a long rectangular present. Cathy opened it. It was a wooden snowflake mobile in a clear plastic box. 'It's for hanging over the baby's cot,' Millie said. 'I had it sent over from America. Isn't it adorable?'

'Thanks, Millie.' Another kiss.

Pam handed Cathy an envelope. 'I got this in Wicklow,' she said with a grin. 'Sorry it's not more exciting.'

Cathy looked inside. 'A voucher for The Beauty Spot salon in Greystones. Ah, thanks, Pam. Just what I need. I can't touch my feet at this stage and I'd die for a pedicure and some red nail polish. I hate bare toenails in the summer.'

'I'm glad you like it,' Pam said.

'I love it, thanks.' Cathy beamed and blew her a kiss.

The other women gave Cathy their gifts – a new Marian Keyes novel, massage oil, scented candles, a T-shirt saying 'Mum's the Word'. By the end of it all, I was feeling very left out.

'So what did you get Cathy, Amy?' Lisa asked me in front of everyone after the last present had been opened.

'Amy gave me the best present of all,' Cathy said. 'A whole weekend away without the children. She's going to mind Arthur and Anna for me next weekend.'

Pam gasped. 'Oh, you lucky thing. How sweet of you, Amy. Why didn't I think of that?'

'That's the best present ever,' Polly agreed. 'Lucky you, Cathy.'

Lisa and Millie looked very miffed.

'And now,' Cathy said, standing up, 'who'd like coffee?'

When Cathy had left the room, Lisa walked towards me. 'Clever present,' she said. 'But have you any experience looking after children, Amy? It's a big responsibility.'

'I know that,' I said.

'And Arthur is a handful,' she added.

'Amy will be great,' Pam said, sticking up for me. 'Just great.'

I hoped she was right. I was a bit worried, to be honest.

Pam patted my arm. 'Bring lots of sweets and chocolate as bribes for

Arthur,' she said, 'and you'll be fine. Don't tell Cathy I said so. And he loves Batman,' she added. 'You could rent the Batman movies. Cathy doesn't let him watch anything violent, so don't tell her. But they're all pretty harmless. I've watched them with the kids myself.'

'Good idea.' I liked Pam. She was like my partner in crime.

# Ten

A little later, I was waiting upstairs to use the toilet when I heard light footsteps coming up the stairs. It was Lisa's little girl, Lizzie.

'Are you all right, Lizzie?' I asked kindly. 'Looking for your mummy?'

Lizzie looked up at me with her cornflower-blue eyes. She had perfect skin with rosy cheeks. She was a very attractive child and she knew it. 'She's in there with Millie,' Lizzie said, pointing at the door of Anna's bedroom. 'She said not to go in.' Lizzie was jigging up and down and clutching her white muslin dress in front of her stomach.

'Do you need to use the toilet?'

Lizzie nodded.

Just then the toilet door opened. Pam came out. 'Sorry, guys. Didn't realise there was a queue. It's all yours.'

'Thanks. Lizzie, do you need any help?' I asked. She ran past us and slammed the door closed in our faces.

'Obviously not,' Pam laughed. 'Charming child. See you downstairs, Amy. And don't let Millie and Lisa get to you. They can be terribly catty at times. Just ignore them.'

'I will. Thanks.'

As Pam walked down the stairs, I wondered what Lisa and Millie were actually doing in Anna's bedroom. It was a little strange. Curiosity got the better of me. I tiptoed towards the door, put my ear against it and strained to listen. Nothing. If they weren't talking, what were they at? Maybe Lizzie had got it wrong. Maybe they were actually downstairs or in the garden.

Lizzie opened the bathroom door and stared at me. I jumped back from the door and tried to look innocent.

'Can I go in there?' Lizzie asked, pointing at the door. 'I'm bored. There are no nice toys in this house, only baby toys. I want my Barbies. And the food is yuck.'

'I don't see why not,' I said. I smiled encouragingly at the rude little girl. 'Go ahead.'

Lizzie pulled on the door handle and pushed the door wide open.

I couldn't believe my eyes. Lisa and Millie were entwined in a passionate embrace, lips locked together.

'Mummy,' Lizzie said running towards Lisa.

Millie and Lisa jumped apart. Millie's pale face blushed deeply. Lisa looked just as flustered.

'What are you doing in here, Lizzie?' Lisa demanded. 'I told you to stay downstairs. Mummy's busy.'

Very busy, I thought to myself.

'Why were you kissing Millie, Mummy?' Lisa asked innocently.

'I was just making her better,' Lisa said quickly. 'Now go back downstairs. I'll be down in a minute, OK?'

'Can I have some crisps?' Lizzie asked, narrowing her eyes. She knew when her mum was trying to get rid of her. And she was extremely good at taking advantage of it. She was her mother's daughter, after all. 'There are crisps on the grown-ups' table. And biscuits.'

'Have whatever you like,' Lisa said. 'Just go downstairs.'

Lizzie skipped off happily.

I stood looking at the two women, a smile playing on my lips. 'Well, well,' I said finally. 'Who would have thought?'

'You won't tell anyone?' Millie asked anxiously. 'It's only a silly little experiment. Nothing serious.'

Lisa glared at Millie.

'Well, it is, isn't it?' Millie asked.

Lisa's face was like thunder. She stormed past us and down the stairs.

'Looks like you've upset your girlfriend,' I said, trying to suppress a giggle.

'Don't call her that,' Millie insisted. 'Please don't say anything to anyone, Amy. Please? I'm so embarrassed. It won't happen again. I just wanted to see what it was like.'

'And Lisa?'

Millie shrugged. 'Have you ever met her husband?'

I shook my head.

'Well if you had, you'd understand. Horrible man. Can't blame her for looking for some affection. He's always working. Has a mistress too. I just felt sorry for her. Please, promise me you won't say anything?'

I thought for a moment. 'I might. Then again I might not. It depends.'

'Please,' Millie begged again. 'I'll do anything. Please …'

# Eleven

'Anita, you'll never guess what happened at Cathy's lunch earlier.' I sat back in the sofa and wound the telephone wire around my fingers. I'd just got in and I was dying to tell her the news. I'd already tried Cathy's phone, but it was engaged. I didn't get a chance to talk to her earlier in private.

'What? Did her brand-new thousand-pound curtains fall down? Or did one of her posh Waterford Crystal glasses break?'

'Anita!'

'Sorry, I shouldn't be so catty. She's just so perfect, it makes me spit.'

'Actually, Cathy's going to retrain as a baby masseuse. She's bored at home. She wants to do something for herself. She's going to take a baby massage course in town. Then she's going to set up her own classes for mothers in the Wicklow area after she's had the baby. To be honest, I think she needs to get some of her old self-confidence back. I think she feels a little faceless at the moment.'

'Really? She always seems very happy with her lot to me.'

'Appearances can be deceptive,' I said. 'Money isn't everything, you know.'

'I suppose not. Listen, tell Cathy I hope her course goes well. And tell her if she needs any help later on with advertising her classes ...'

'Do you really mean that?'

'Of course. Why not? I could put a sign up in the bookshop and help her print up some flyers. And you could write a piece on the classes for *Ruby*.'

'Good idea. Thanks for being so supportive.'

'She's your friend, after all, so she can't be all that bad. I didn't realise she was unhappy. It just goes to show – you never know what goes on behind closed doors.'

'You have a good heart, Anita.' I smiled. I was lucky to have them both as friends. And maybe Cathy and Anita would finally start getting along. Stranger things had happened. It would certainly make my life a whole lot easier.

'Speaking of closed doors,' I said, 'wait till I tell you. But you have to promise to keep it a secret, OK? I have to tell someone or I'll burst.'

'Sounds interesting.'

'Interesting is an understatement, Anita. It's dynamite! But you have to swear on Johnny Depp's life.' Anita worshipped Johnny Depp.

'OK. I swear. But it had better be good.'

# Twelve

The following morning, Kitty looked up at me over her trendy half-moon glasses. 'Amy, we'd like to offer you the staff job at *Ruby* if you're interested. You have a good, solid CV. You're not afraid to go after the big stories. We were most impressed with the Rex O'Hara interview,' she added. 'Most impressed. How did you wangle that? He gave only one other interview to the Irish press and that was to *The Irish Times*.'

'Contacts,' I smiled, giving nothing away. Rex had been utterly charming. He'd remembered his first interview with *Ruby* all those years ago. He was happy to talk to me.

'Gets me out of an awful family do,' he'd said. 'Daisy's family are painful.'

I'd laughed.

I said nothing to Rex about Millie, his sister-in-law to be. And about her clinch with Lisa. I'd made a promise, after all, to keep their little secret. And you have to keep promises and secrets. Except from your best friends, of course – like Anita and Cathy.

I still hadn't talked to Cathy yet. I couldn't wait to tell her the news about my staff job at *Ruby*. And about what goes on behind closed doors!

# OPEN DOOR SERIES

*continued overleaf*

*Has Anyone Here Seen Larry?*
by Deirdre Purcell

## SERIES FOUR

*The Story of Joe Brown* by Rose Doyle
*Stray Dog* by Gareth O'Callaghan
*The Smoking Room* by Julie Parsons
*World Cup Diary* by Niall Quinn
*Fair-Weather Friend* by Patricia Scanlan
*The Quiz Master* by Michael Scott

## SERIES FIVE

*Mrs Whippy* by Cecelia Ahern
*The Underbury Witches* by John Connolly
*Mad Weekend* by Roddy Doyle
*Not a Star* by Nick Hornby
*Secrets* by Patricia Scanlan
*Behind Closed Doors* by Sarah Webb

TRADE/CREDIT CARD ORDERS TO:
*CMD, 55A Spruce Avenue,*
*Stillorgan Industrial Park,*
*Blackrock, Co. Dublin, Ireland.*
*Tel: (+353 1) 294 2560*
*Fax: (+353 1) 294 2564*


TO PLACE PERSONAL/EDUCATIONAL
ORDERS OR TO ORDER A CATALOGUE
PLEASE CONTACT:
*New Island, 2 Brookside,*
*Dundrum Road, Dundrum,*
*Dublin 14, Ireland.*
*Tel: (+353 1) 298 6867/298 3411*
*Fax: (+353 1) 298 7912*
www.newisland.ie